WAY OF THE ODYSSEY SHORT STORY COLLECTION VOLUME 2

CONNOR WHITELEY

No part of this book may be reproduced in any form or by any electronic or mechanical means. Including information storage, and retrieval systems, without written permission from the author except for the use of brief quotations in a book review.

This book is NOT legal, professional, medical, financial or any type of official advice.

Any questions about the book, rights licensing, or to contact the author, please email connorwhiteley@connorwhiteley.net

Copyright © 2024 CONNOR WHITELEY

All rights reserved.

DEDICATION
Thank you to all my readers without you I couldn't do what I love.

SOCIALLY CRIMINAL

Justice Aisha Roar sat on her favourite cold, damp and sticky wooden bar stool in the messy Public House just off Main Street in the heart of the criminal underworld. The light was dark, scary and criminally good just how she liked it and the pub was thankfully filled with her favourite people tonight.

She sat towards the back like she always did and she pressed her black-armoured back against the sticky wooden walls that stunk of cheap alcohol, sex and sweat, just like how a good pub should smell. There were a few floating orbs of light swimming around against the dirty black ceiling providing just enough light, but it wasn't like anyone here actually wanted to see anyone's faces.

Everyone here was just here to drink, be merry and maybe have some random sex because it just felt good in the moment.

Aisha had always loved her time here and the constant background noise of people talking, laughing and shouting made her thinly smile. It was always great to be here after a long day of hunting down criminals and killing them because that was the law, but she always loved a good drink even more.

There was a brand-new wooden stage up at the front of the pub which Aisha really didn't like, because there was some hip-pop rubbish band from Earth playing there.

Aisha really didn't know what crime those fools had committed to end up in some junk bar like this one. The musicians were good, damn good so Aisha just couldn't understand whatsoever why these people wanted to play here.

They could easily get thousands of Rexes and then even more through tips if they played in the Spires, where the posh people lived. So maybe their crime was just stupidity and Aisha was half tempted to donate some of her money to them but she had already met her personal monthly quota of charity giving.

And she wouldn't want to get a foul reputation as a do-gooder. She actually shuddered at the very idea.

A cute young couple walked past her table, the woman looked okay wearing a very short black skirt, and the young man looked stunning in his tight jeans, shirt and boots. Hopefully both of them were in for a lucky night tonight, but Aisha was still alone.

Most of the Justices on the planet preferred to be alone because it was what their job required, each Justice was a law onto themselves and no one except the Glorious Rex himself on Earth could ever challenge their judgement.

It didn't make dating easy, it certainly made having a family impossible but Aisha still loved her job. It was her small way of helping to make the Imperium a better place with less freaks, criminals and alien scum in it.

"Lady Justice," a man said coming over to the table.

Aisha rolled her eyes. As much as she loved helping people, donating secretly to charities and making the Imperium a safer place, everyone knew never to disturb a Justice when they were drinking.

There might not have been a lot of social activity in the Imperium outside of work, watching fights and gambling, but drinking was a sacred activity of the Justices.

"I was hoping to have a moment of your time in exchange for this," the man said.

A small floating orb of light hovered over head and Aisha had a feeling that the owner of the pub was watching her, technically illegally but privacy was a joke these days.

Aisha focused on the small crystal glass of golden liquid and she instantly knew it was a very fine whiskey not found on this planet. That had to have cost the man a few thousand Rexes, so why was he giving it to her?

Aisha looked at the man and he was surprisingly

young with smooth sexy features, a pretty face and his slim body looked amazing in his tight robes denoting he was from the local College.

Definitely a man that did not belong in the deepest, darkest depths of this planet.

"Are there not Justices at the Colleges? In the Spires? In your own family?" Aisha asked.

The floating orb of light dipped a little lower and if it dared to get much closer then Aisha would happily smash it. What could the owner of the pub do? Call the Justices?

"Of course but I require a more roguish touch for my problem and I know you have a very effective reputation for getting rid of people," the man said.

Aisha had to admit she loved how her reputation was finally taking shape but she really didn't want this young man thinking that Justices were dangerous, it was the criminals they hunted that they were the real danger. Then she just smiled because the constant indoctrination that all subjects of the Imperium went through should take care of that.

"Of course, if your target has committed a crime then they will die. That is the law. If they steal a slice of bread, they die. If they assault someone, they die. If they murder someone, they die," Aisha said.

The young man frowned a little. "My wedding application got denied recently and I want you to fix it,"

Aisha smiled. It was a great effective feature of the Imperium that in order for two people to get married the Rex had to personally approve it and even then they could only get married if it served the Imperium.

A lot of maths, statistics and problem-solving was used to calculate how great the marriage would impact the Imperium and most of the time marriages were accepted. It was important to the fabric of society that the rich only married the rich, doctors only married doctors and the poor only married the poor. It was critical to stop the corrupting influence of the lower classes from ruining the rich people that were actually going to make something of themselves.

Aisha wasn't always sure she agreed with but it was an interesting idea.

"The Rex made his decision, even a Justice cannot overrule them. What were the stated reasons?" Aisha asked.

"I cannot marry my girlfriend because I am a student and she is a military Commander two years older than me,"

Aisha nodded. That was strange and it meant that the girlfriend had to come from a military family to get promoted that quickly. But students and military types were always marrying.

Except when one thing was revealed.

"What are you studying in?" Aisha asked.

The man smiled and Aisha smiled too. He was clearly passionate about it, so it had to be something grand like the military, sciences, medicine or a whole host of other brilliant subjects.

"I'm studying game design," the man said.

Aisha just reached across the table, grabbed the man's whiskey and downed it in one.

There was nothing kind she could say to the man because game design was useless to helping the Imperium survived so he was a useless man. But it was clear as day that he loved the subject.

And Aisha had always respected passion.

"And I refused to take the propaganda module," the man said.

Out of instinct Aisha moved her hand down to her waist where her gun was but she stopped her. This young man wasn't a radical that was a danger to the Imperium. He was just a young man that wanted to marry his girlfriend.

He did not need to die no matter how many of her peers would have killed him for not helping the Imperium indoctrinate young minds through games.

That was actually a crime so technically she had to kill this young man but she wanted to learn more and help him.

And if she found more evidence of his crimes against the Imperium then she would sadly have to kill him.

"I've come to you because the personal reference on my marriage application lied about me," the man said.

Aisha leant forward. Now that was a much more serious crime.

"What's your name?" Aisha asked as she stood up and downed the rest of her drink in one.

"Joshua Laurie," he said.

Aisha grabbed him and took him out of the pub. "Well Joshua, take me to this liar and then we will see how he committed the most outrageous crime imaginable. They lied to the Glorious Rex himself,"

Aisha felt so excited as they left the pub because she was finally going to hunt down her criminal.

A criminal that might need the ultimate punishment.

***

Aisha was hardly surprised too much when Joshua led her down through the dirty, stinky and toxic narrow streets of the criminal underworld with her fingers tightly on the trigger of her gun.

Then Joshua led her into a very crawl and dirty metal chamber inside an abandoned building. The chamber itself was immense covered with black mouldy walls, puddles of stagnant water covered the floor as did streaks of brown dried blood.

Aisha just smiled as she watched two very attractive middle-aged men clearing up after the fight that had caused the streaks of blood, and judging by the sheer amount of holo-cigars, bullets and broken weapons there must have been a hell of a crowd here tonight.

There were only three social activities in all of the Imperium. There was drinking which Aisha loved, there was watching or taking part in fights or there was gambling. Aisha really didn't like the last two because she preferred fighting on the streets (illegal to all but Justices) and gambling was just stupid.

But judging by the chamber some people seriously loved watching a good fight.

"This is the man that lied on my application," Joshua said pointing to one of the two middle-aged men.

Aisha pointed her gun at him and just focused on how disgusting he looked in his dirty cloak, soaked-through boots and blackened teeth.

"Why the hell did you want this man on your wedding application?" Aisha asked.

"Because I'm his father," the man said.

Aisha just shook her head. There really was no ending to humanity's stupidity and it made no sense how this man working in the criminal underworld had managed to get a son into a local College. That should have been impossible.

Aisha made a note to herself to investigate the College tomorrow. There was no telling if Joshua's criminal family might have started corrupting the rich students of the College.

"Why did you lie dad on my application? I saw it and you said I was unfaithful to my girlfriend and I had donated to pro-Keres charities,"

Aisha pointed the gun at the son. The Keres were foul alien abominations that wanted to destroy humanity and their way of life. It was an awful crime to help them.

"Relax Lady Justice, he did no such thing," the father said.

Aisha decided to put her gun away because these two people made no sense and their actions literally went against how the Imperium worked.

"How are you two even related? There are strict laws against poor degenerates going to College. How did you get in?" Aisha asked.

Joshua smiled. "My girlfriend pulled a few strings and got me into college. I rose up through the class quickly and effectively and now I'm on the Student Council,"

As much as Aisha wanted to be annoyed that a poor person had a position of power in the local College, she actually couldn't be annoyed. The man was clearly intelligent, kind and passionate and of course Aisha would never admit this to her peers but the Imperium needed more people like that.

And so many of the laws were just dumb social laws to control others that it was just so stupid.

Poor people needed to go to College, get educated and help the Imperium, because the rich people were hardly doing an amazing job.

The father came over to Aisha. "Please don't arrest me and my son. We're good people, I provide innocent workers with sanctioned entertainment and that is what my son wants to do. We want to be entertainers, not criminals,"

All of Aisha's instincts, training and textbooks were telling her to just kill these two people now because they were a theoretical threat to the Imperium, but they weren't.

They seriously weren't.

Aisha knew that the father just wanted to entertain people as did the son just through different methods, but there was still one important question left.

"Why didn't you want your son getting married?" Aisha asked.

The father looked at the ground focusing on a long streak of blood that looked impossible to clean.

"I wanted my son to marry who he actually loves. He doesn't love the military girl, they both only wanted sex from each other and they were both using each other,"

Aisha looked at Joshua. "Is this true?"

Joshua nodded like he was proud of it. "Yeah. She wanted to have sex with a poor degenerate for the thrill and I wanted to go to College. I wanted her as much as she wanted me but when her father started asking questions she wanted to get married to protect herself,"

"And you didn't?" Aisha asked.

Joshua nodded and Aisha had to admit it was nice when the father hugged his son, that was a rare sight these days in the Imperium. A very unfortunate day.

As Aisha just looked at the father and son she

couldn't deny how badly the law said they both had to die. The father had lied to the Rex himself, the son had illegally gone to College and used a military girl for his own gain (a strange little law made that illegal) and even the girlfriend needed to die technically because she had been having sex outside her permissible social rank.

It was all so stupid and as much as it would end Aisha's life, career and drinking fund if anyone found out she simply lowered her gun and walked away.

There were no crimes here, not real ones anyway, and all these social crimes were all victimless but Aisha still had to investigate the College just in case.

But she really, really hoped that Joshua would find happiness because it was the very least that everyone deserved.

***

Aisha had loved stalking the long perfectly clean, refreshingly nutty-scented air of the local College as she had investigated for any sign of corruption amongst the local rich students, and thankfully there had been none. In fact they seemed to be even more dedicated and indoctrinated into the Imperial Cult that worshipped everything the Rex said as divine law.

That was brilliant for the sake of the Imperium.

As Aisha sat later that night at the back of the bar again resting her black armour against the wooden sticky walls and her hands wrapped around a wonderfully cold tankard of beer, she was really happy with herself.

Because by proving that the law was wrong about the strict social controls of the Imperium, maybe she could get them to be dropped as laws and then the Rex's plans for mass indoctrination could be even stronger, better and more effective so no one could ever question the righteousness of his rule.

Then maybe there would be less criminals and that meant more drinking time in this great pub. Aisha really did enjoy the constant sweet aromas of sweat, stale beer and sex, there was just nothing else like it.

And in a cold, unloving galaxy, Aisha knew that love was always needed and now Joshua was alive and free to find who he loved and hopefully Aisha could find someone to love her in the end.

She smiled at that, that really would be an amazing thing to have.

But until then would always be more criminals, more murders and thieves to find, investigate and kill and that seriously excited Aisha a lot more than she ever wanted to admit.

BATTLE DOCTRINES

Ship Mistress Olivia Flapper stood on her raised metal platform in the middle of her white spherical bridge on her great warship *Rex's Hammer*. She had always wanted to be a Ship Mistress, a great leader of the Imperium's war efforts and now after so many years of service, fighting and political workings she was finally one of them.

The bridge was still brand-new to Olivia but it was as wonderful as she ever could have imagined. She really liked the spherical shape of the walls, its smooth white metal was a little too shiny in places but she would sort it all out in time.

Her small raised platform was only big enough for her to stand on which was absolutely perfect, especially as Olivia wasn't a fan of the constant smells of body odour, sweat and blood that seemed to pour off her command crew like rain from a duck. It wasn't exactly pleasant.

At least the small bright golden orbs of light

bounced around the bridge, bouncing from one wall to another and back again.

Sometimes when Olivia was alone (which wasn't as often as she would have liked) she just stared at the little orbs. Sometimes they were happier, freer and more content with life than she was.

As much as Olivia loved her new position, her service to the Rex and her life, she just felt like there was more to life than always searching for the next promotion and intensely studying the next battle doctrine that old men with no military experience had created.

The circular warship hummed loudly and Olivia looked down at her command crew, all twenty of them, as they were hunched over their large bulky metal computer screens having to have computations by hand, having to calculate their trajectory by hand and having to inform different departments of the warship by hand.

This certainly wasn't the most modern ship she had ever been on but it was customary for all brand-new Ship Masters and Mistresses to get put on the lowest ships first of all. Apparently it was so they could develop their skills, but Olivia knew it was because the new ones were the most likely to die so it was cheaper to put them on poorer ships before "gifting" them the more expensive warships.

She wasn't really a fan of that rule.

Olivia waved at her command crew as they

walked about or did their work wearing their long white robes denoting their position and their newness to the role. It was a shame that Olivia was surrounded by newbies judging by their bright white robes without a single speck of dirt on them.

Either they were so new that they had only graduated from the academy in the past two days or the environmental systems were *so* good that they seriously purified the air.

Judging by the rest of the ship, Olivia fully believed it was the former.

"Ship Mistress, we're detecting three enemy ships incoming. Within firing distance in five minutes," a very short man said with a balding head.

Olivia nodded slowly and her hands tightened around the cold metal railings of her raised platform. She had been sent here on this mission to deliver bombs to a faraway planet to help Imperial forces annihilate a rogue cult of Dark Keres, but clearly the enemy didn't want these bombs delivered.

She had no idea what separated the Dark Keres to the rest of their foul, magic freaks of their Keres species. The Treaty of Defeat was such a weak little treaty that might have meant the awful Keres species was starving itself to death but the Dark Keres were awful.

Unlike the normal Keres, these so-called Dark Keres actually had a spine and they were fighting back against the righteousness of humanity. It was humanity's Rex-given right to rule the stars, purge entire species and claim all the planets they wanted.

And it was the Keres's duty to die or at least join humanity as slaves as so many of their foul kind had.

Olivia focused on the icy coldness of space dead away from them as two large holographic screens appeared showing Olivia the endless blackness of space with no nearby planets, imperial forces or stars close by.

They were alone.

Olivia really didn't want to fight these Dark Keres because they might have been breaking the law time after time but they were just trying to do what they could to survive.

Humanity was constantly doing questionable things to make sure it survived, so maybe the Keres' weren't so different from them after all.

"Battle Doctrine Mistress," a very tall woman said.

Olivia bit her lip as she couldn't even see the foul enemy ships yet, she didn't know what Dark Keres ships looked like but she was going to have to proceed as her training suggested she should.

"Advancement Battle Doctrine," Olivia said.

As the bridge became a hive of activity with her command crew running round like headless chickens, she had to admit it wasn't her favourite Doctrine.

The Advancement Doctrine was sadly all about travelling quickly through space to make sure the enemy couldn't catch up with them. It meant deactivating the weapon systems to give the engines more power but hopefully it would still work.

Olivia really wanted to see the enemy but she just couldn't.

The Keres were masters of their magic and it was so damn annoying that they were probably using it to cloak their ships. For all Olivia knew they could be right next to them.

"How did you know the Keres were here in the first place?" Olivia asked.

None of the command crew were paying attention to her as the warship hummed, banged and vibrated as the engines were given more power. She hated this.

Olivia had fought the Keres plenty of times and whilst the Dark Keres might be different to the rest of their race, she was still willing to bet that they used the same or similar tactics.

The Keres were waiting to ambush them and she feared that the Advancement Doctrine was exactly what they wanted.

"We found them on the edge of the system for a brief second before they cloaked themselves," a woman said as she rushed past.

Olivia nodded but it made no sense. The Keres knew that they couldn't outgun, beat or destroy an Imperial warship because they were so weak, so why in the Rex's fine name did they reveal themselves?

Unless it was all part of a plan.

It was moments like this that just made Olivia

want to jump into Ultraspace and zoom through the galaxy at light speed regardless of how apparently dangerous that was with the bombs.

She just wanted to keep her crew alive, and herself of course.

"Scan the surrounding area," Olivia said.

Only one man looked up at her but he shrugged as he ran the scan and then shook his head at her.

Olivia's heart pounded in her chest. She was used to dealing with impossible humans, impossible tasks and impossible crew members. She wasn't used to dealing with impossible aliens.

She didn't want her crew to die. She didn't want to fail. She had to deliver the bombs to the planet over ten hours away.

Then Olivia realised that sometimes the Keres did a little trick where they magically project their ships into space to make the Imperium believe they were in one location when they were actually in another.

The enemy was a lot closer than Olivia ever wanted to admit.

Then Olivia felt her skin turn icy cold and she had only ever had that reaction once. Seconds before the Keres attacked her in the most violent way possible.

"Invasion Doctrine!" Olivia shouted.

But it was too late.

The ship jerked.

Throwing Olivia across the bridge.

Other crew members smashed around her.

Bodies shattering.

Streaks of blood painting the walls.

Alarms screamed overhead.

Flashing lights exploded on.

Olivia forced herself up. She forced herself towards her raised platform.

Her body screamed in protest but she accessed her private hologram.

She saw thousands of victims all over the ship from the impact. A bomb had hit their starboard side but their shields were intact and their anti-magic systems were okay.

At least the Keres couldn't teleport or board them for now.

The two massive holograms that showed her the darkness of space earlier now showed three immense dagger-like warships with blood red crystal hulls appear next to her.

Olivia couldn't believe that the damn Dark Keres were right next to them. That was the last thing she wanted.

She had to somehow figure out a way to keep herself and her crew alive and how to get the bombs to the battlefleet.

For the briefest of moments Olivia supposed she could activate the bombs right now and just kill them all and the Keres warships next to her. But she didn't want to use the No Hope Doctrine just yet.

She wouldn't dare give the alien abominations some reward for their attack. Olivia was going to win no matter what it took.

"Mistress," a voice said but Olivia didn't bother to see who it was. "The Keres want to contact us. They're requesting we surrender to them,"

Olivia shook her head. These damn aliens were never going to get her to surrender.

Olivia forced herself upright and she gripped the metal railings of her raised platform and frowned at the two holographic screens showing the enemy warships.

"We need to activate the weapon systems immediately," Olivia said.

"It will do us no good. The enemy are on the starboard side and our weapons on that side are destroyed," a man said.

Olivia couldn't believe how damn infuriating these aliens were. And the man was right sadly.

A loud humming of pure magical energy crackled around her and Olivia rolled her eyes as the damn anti-magic systems were failing. It wouldn't be too long now until the Keres invaded and slaughtered them all like the beasts they were.

Olivia opened a ship-wide communication channel. "All forces this is the Ship Mistress enact the Containment Doctrine immediately. Do not allow a witch to live,"

Olivia just shook her head even more as her

command crew all bit their lower lip. They all knew this was bad because if the anti-magic generators collapsed then the Keres would easily rip into reality and stalk the holy halls of their warship.

And they would kill human after human until they all died.

The Containment Doctrine was simple but useless. A simple hell mary to throw into the air to buy Olivia some more time.

"What about the engines?" Olivia asked.

A young woman from the crew stepped forward. "Contained by Keres. They're using our magic to immobilise them. I could undo the magic but it would take time,"

"How much?"

"Ten minutes," she said.

The air crackled and murderous screams echoed around the ship.

"Do it," Olivia said to the woman before turning to her crew. "Connect me to Keres ships. I'll buy us some time. Weapons won't free us here. Words might,"

Olivia could literally feel the tension in the bridge now and she wanted to slice it with a sword but she had to focus and remain strong. Some Keres creatures only needed eye contact to use their magic.

Olivia had to focus and not allow the abominations to use their magic on her.

Moments later a very tall, thin elf-like woman appeared in blue holographic form with very long golden black hair that flowed around her like angelic wings.

"You must hand over your weapons please my friend," the woman said. "My forces want to unleash their Death Magic on you but I am buying you time,"

Olivia grinned. The woman's voice was very elegant, lyrical and perfect but she was just stupid. Olivia was a Ship Mistress of the Imperium, she did not listen to the lies and deceits and corruption that aliens spread.

And she wasn't going to give them anything.

As soon as the engines were free once more she was going to escape and jump into Ultraspace and to hell with the consequences.

"I will not give you a damn thing alien. These bombs will reach the planet and they will be dropped on your kind and then humanity will rule the stars," Olivia said.

She wasn't exactly sure if she believed it and she didn't know if the Keres on the planet deserved to die but she wanted to act tough at least.

Olivia noticed the female Keres was looking at someone else probably behind the hologram then the female Keres nodded.

"Then you leave me no choice and I know your workers are trying to free the engines," she said.

The entire command crew went still but Olivia waved them to continue.

"Let me show you just a touch of our Death

Magic," the woman said before uttering strange twisted words in a tongue Olivia didn't understand or care to listen to.

Olivia cut the transmission but when she looked back at her command crew they were all wide-eyed with terror as they stared back at their computer screens.

Olivia climbed down and looked at the silent ghostly pictures of their friends, fellow crew members and even loved ones turn to black crystal before shattering into dust.

"Two percent of the crew is dead," someone said but Olivia didn't care who.

"Are the engines free?" Olivia asked.

"Almost," a woman said.

Olivia climbed back up to her raised platform and contacted the Keres warships again.

"Did you like my gift? I know the Goddess of Souls was particularly happy," the female Keres said.

Olivia's hands formed fists. She seriously didn't care for the strange alien mythology of the Keres.

The air charged with magic energy and Olivia felt the icy coldness of the Keres's foul touch around her. They were within striking distance.

She just had to buy her crew a little more time.

"Does your Goddess love Keres souls?" Olivia asked.

The female Keres laughed. "Souls are souls my dear. I'll let you meet her now. Because now you die!"

An alien claw formed in the air.

Slashing at Olivia.

She stumbled back.

The claw chased her.

Olivia leapt off her platform.

She smashed onto the floor.

The claw lashed at her.

Olivia rolled forward.

Another claw appeared in front of her.

Olivia jumped to one side.

She hit a table.

The two claws flew at her.

The ship jerked.

The engines were free.

"Into Ultraspace!" Olivia shouted.

The entire ship screamed in protest.

The Keres were trying to anchor them into reality.

Olivia whipped out her pistol.

She shot the two claws.

They disappeared.

The warship zoomed off into Ultraspace and all Olivia could think about was how badly she didn't want the bombs to explode.

***

Olivia absolutely had to admit that the next hour was the longest one of her entire life, each second she was half-expecting one of her crew to shout that the bombs were overheating or somehow having a reaction to Ultraspace travel.

Thankfully they weren't.

Olivia just smiled as she leant against the warm metal railings of her raised platform and watched as the streaks of purple light from the Ultraspace network tunnel (she really didn't know how it worked) zoomed past her.

Then with a quiet thud the tunnel disappeared and Olivia was so damn happy that she was alive and that her crew were okay. Then the entire ship hummed a little as an Imperial network connected to her ship and took control of the bombs.

For a small moment Olivia thought that the Dark Keres had followed her but everyone knew that the Keres were too dumb to use Ultraspace and they stuck with their clearly inferior Nexus System of their own magical creation.

Olivia didn't know how it worked and she didn't want to know. The Keres were dumb, end of story.

And as she watched on the two massive holograms the Imperial fleet zooming around an orange green planet with Keres ships trying to flee, she grinned as the bombs rushed towards the planet ready to be used exactly where they were needed most.

Olivia still wasn't sure if this was just, needed or even right but she hadn't examined the facts of the battle and in all fairness it hadn't mattered.

As much as she didn't like to admit it, the military wasn't designed to produce thinkers, it was designed to produce soldiers that could pick up a gun and march to the beat of the Rex's eternal war machine so humanity could be kept safe, secured and all the enemies could be killed.

The laughter, cheering and even some happy dances filled the bridge as the command crew and everyone else on the ship was so happy to be alive and Olivia was definitely going to join them later on.

She might have doomed a lot of aliens to death but she had helped to protect humanity, her crew and the future of the Imperium. That was certainly a job very well.

And with thousands of other battlefields spread out across the galaxy, Olivia was really excited about flying away from here and seeing what other great adventures, herself, her crew and her great lower warship could travel to.

Then maybe, just maybe Olivia could finally get a promotion and get a real warship because as she had survived this adventure Olivia was fairly sure she could survive anything.

And that was a great realisation to have and that was all thanks to her battle doctrines.

COMMUNICATING IN ULTRASPACE

This was the day he died.

Chief Communication Officer Grayson Jones sat on a large grey metal table that was surprisingly smooth, shiny and very relaxing oddly enough. It was almost strange for a table in his little metal boxroom of a break room to be so relaxing and well-maintained. Normally when he worked on ships the breakrooms were so dilapidated that they were just flat out disgusting.

Thankfully everything about the brand-new black circular ship imaginatively called the *Communication* was up to date, clean and perfectly maintained. Grayson had already been on the ship for two weeks and he had yet to find a single problem with the ship.

The only problem with the ship was that it was the smooth walls of the break room were just so plain and dull. Grayson wanted to splash some colour on the walls and maybe hang a few pictures. A nice red, blue or orange might have looked nice and it would be a nice reminder of his homeworld.

Grayson really liked that idea as he wrapped his rough hand around his coffee mug, the sharp bitter taste of it was one of the highlights of living on the ships. And it helped to provide a brief distraction against the overwhelming aromas of roasted peaches, sweat and salted peanuts that clung to everything in the corridor amongst the ship.

He didn't know why the environmental systems were so obsessed with the smell, they could have been faulty, but it was rather nice at first before getting old real quick.

At least the job was simple enough, he was just in charge of making sure all the equipment ran smoothly so all the nearby Imperial forces could route their communications through his station, before the ship blasted the messages off through Ultraspace towards their destination.

Ultraspace was amazing and Grayson really loved learning about it at university. It was just stunning how humanity had managed to create or tap into an intergalactic network of tunnels that allowed for faster-than-light travel.

It was simply brilliant.

And the only thing Grayson needed to do was keep it all working otherwise he absolutely hated to imagine what would happen if he failed. Battle orders might not be read or sent, distress calls might not be heard and vital intelligence might not be known about aliens and terrorists.

If Grayson failed then he sadly knew a lot of good people could die and there was no way he was ever allowing himself to have that on his conscious. He didn't volunteer for five years in the Peace Corps to allow innocent people to die.

"We have a problem," a woman said as a large circular door opened with an annoying screaming sound that almost made Grayson jump.

He looked at the Chief of Engineering, a beautiful woman called Mary wearing a very attractive pink blouse, trousers and white trainers.

But if she was coming to him then it had to be bad.

"What happened this time?" Grayson asked grinning.

"The Ultraspace generator died," Mary said plainly.

Grayson just shook his head. Of all the damn things that could possibly go wrong, he seriously didn't want this to be the problem.

Without their Ultraspace generator then the ship couldn't run away or travel through the network basically increasing their travel time by a factor of 100 and that meant the Ultraspace Communicator would fail sooner or later too.

Grayson had sadly worked too many jobs where the failing of the Ultraspace generator wasn't seen as the first sign of an Ultraspace shutdown on the ship so when the damn aliens attacked. There was no way of escape or call for help.

Those people always died.

"And there's ten Keres ships two systems over. The great benefits of invading their territory," Mary said.

Grayson seriously didn't want to attract the attention of the foul alien beasts with their awful magic. He wanted to escape in short order and he hardly agreed with Mary about space being the Keres' domain. The stars belonged to humanity and only humanity.

"I presume you've tried turning it on and off?" Grayson asked.

Mary playfully hit him over the head. "I didn't come to you to get mocked. This is a communicator error, the Ultraspace Communicator is *telling* the Generator to shut down,"

Grayson leant forward. He had heard a hell of a lot of things in his decades of service as a soldier fighting the Keres and then even more as a communication specialist. He had never heard of pieces of the ship *telling* each other what to do.

He wasn't even sure if the Keres's magic could do such things to Imperial ships.

"Take me there immediately please," Grayson said.

He was surprised at how hesitant Mary was to let him go but she nodded after a few seconds and smiled.

"You're going to need an environmental suit. It's pretty nasty in there,"

Grayson hated it how his stomach twisted into a painful knot as he realised that things were going to get a hell of a lot worse before they could ever get better.

***

Grayson had always hated damn environmental suits. He hated their bright red appearance that made him look like a tomato, he hated how his movements were so slow and controlled and he hated how it was always just damn impossible to see out of them.

Even now as he slowly went into the environmentally sealed Ultraspace chamber, an immense black metal chamber with two huge metal tanks containing strange complex technology allowing them to tap into Ultraspace whenever they wanted, Grayson realised just how bad this all actually was.

He had been in chambers like this all over the Imperium and they never changed much but they were always clean, smelt sweet and they always left the taste of lemon drizzle cake on his tongue just like how his father used to make it when he was a child.

But this chamber was simply disgusting with the smell and taste of harsh chemicals, toxic radiation and death filling his senses. His suit's warning systems were already starting to flare to life and no one else knew this but Grayson knew there was a rip in Ultraspace.

He had read about Ultraspace rips plenty of

times and they were always kept under wraps and a strange type of radiation always leaked into the ships and sometimes something worse leaked through with them.

He didn't know what the reports said about the so-called creatures that leaked through the rips but people died and then became ghosts of a fashion. Grayson had no intention of dying today so he looked around for a weapon but there weren't any.

He had thought he was going to die plenty of times in battle, on ships or getting involved in beer brawls. Normally he didn't care about dying as long as it was in service but for some reason he just felt closer to Death than even before.

As Grayson went towards the two metal tanks he could have sworn that he heard laughter and people wanting him to do something. It was like a corrupting chant in the back of his mind urging him to do something dangerous.

He felt the urge to remove his helmet so he could breathe more freely and not have to listen to the constant groan of his breathing but he couldn't.

He had to stay alive or everyone else on the ship might die too.

Grayson took out a smaller scanner that he had picked up on the way over here and he started scanning the chamber and surprisingly enough the Ultraspace Generator was working perfectly.

In fact, everything was apparently working

perfectly, or it was working well enough not to register.

Grayson looked at Mary and just frowned as she had completely removed her environmental suit, her eyes had sunken in on themselves and her feet were now ghostly.

He shook his head as he realised that the rip had corrupted her and she had come to get him because he was the only one that could stop the corruption.

"Death is the ruler of the Network not humanity," Mary said. "Humanity might have wiped out my creations of the Keres but we will rise again,"

Grayson broke out into a fighting position. He had no idea what the hell had corrupted Mary but it was clearly insane.

Sure humanity wanted to obliterate the aliens but they weren't dead yet sadly. So this corrupting creature had to be something to do with their strange alien mythology and abominable magic.

This creature had to die.

The creature infecting Mary just grinned and kept looking at him up and down like he was a piece of meat ready for the slaughter.

Grayson tried to think harder about what had happened to the surviving members of the ships where rips had occurred. He couldn't remember. He knew he had to close the rip but he didn't know how.

He didn't even know how the rips occurred in the first place.

"I see your mind human. You fear me. And just

know that Death grows stronger so your Network will die like your race,"

Mary charged.

Her fingers became swords.

She slashed them.

Grayson rolled to one side.

He couldn't move.

His suit wasn't flexible enough.

He was stuck.

He felt Mary slashed his back.

Grayson screamed as radiation poured into him.

His lungs roared as toxic chemicals filled them.

He screamed as his body turned cancerous.

Every single cell felt like it was fire and then his world went black.

But he knew that he had died for sure.

***

Grayson hated how ghostly, light and strange he felt as he woke up on the bright white floor of an Ultraspace Tunnel. It felt so weird to be inside a tunnel and yet not blinded by its intense white sterile light with a few white circular ships zooming overhead.

The air was unfortunately cold, icy and bitter and Grayson really didn't like how the air smelt of damp, but he just couldn't understand why he was inside a tunnel and not dead-dead.

He looked down at his legs, arms and chest and he bit his lip as he realised that he was like a ghost.

He wasn't completely see-through but he might as well have been.

When he turned around Grayson shook his head as he saw a tear the size of his hand behind him, he went out to touch it but crippling pain filled him. He knew that the rip lead to his ship but he was dead so he could never return.

A strange suckling and humming and buzzing sound came from behind him.

Grayson turned around and he wanted to swear as he saw a very thin shadowy black figure like the Grim Reaper carrying his scythes that Grayson just knew was dripping his own blood.

The figure didn't smile or anything, or maybe he was because Grayson couldn't see his face but the figure was immensely tall, easily five times the height of him. And yet Grayson had no idea what he was.

"I told you I get more and more powerful each day human," the figure said.

"What are you?" Grayson asked. "I don't know you. I don't know who you are. You are nothing to me,"

Grayson guessed that made the Figure smile.

"I am one of the Gods that you claim don't exist. The Keres called me The Destroyer but I prefer the term The Obliterator. Now you have served in your military. You know what I can do?"

Grayson looked to the bright white floor for a moment and he did sort of remember the strange heretical beliefs of the Keres. They believed in a Dark and Light group of gods with The Destroyer being the creator of their Death Magic but they were just myths.

Myths created by a strange doomed dying pathetic race of aliens that humanity would hopefully slaughter one day.

The figure echoed. "Humans are so stupid. You doubt I exist but I feed on your thoughts, your dreams, your ambitions every single time you travel through my network. Do you think it was an accident that your Rex found the Network?"

Grayson nodded.

"Of course not. I grow stronger with more of my Dark Gods are being found and soon I will be free of this prison and soon the galaxy shall burn once again with my rage,"

"Again?" Grayson asked.

The Figure laughed even more. "It is amazing humans can even begin to imagine the grandeur and complexities of the galaxy but I will not tell you anymore. So how about we make a deal?"

Grayson really didn't know what to do about this figure, he was clearly evil, deranged and hellbent on destroying humanity but he could also be a weapon against the Keres. And any weapon against the Keres was a good friend to Grayson.

"Whatever you want," Grayson said.

The Figure laughed as he stretched out a palm without fingers and black energy shot out of them.

The tendrils of black magic swirled, twirled and whirled around Grayson and he screamed in agony for a brief moment as the magic turned him to ash.

But whilst he knew that humanity was ultimately doomed if they didn't learn how to work with the Keres instead of facing them because of the sheer power of the servants of The Destroyer, he knew that his life, knowledge and power was being exchanged for sealing up the rip.

So his friends, crew and ship were now safe and Grayson smiled as he finally became just another white light in the tunnels because he had done his mission, and that would have to be enough for now.

And at least he died in service. Just like he always wanted.

BLACKHEART

Brother meets brother.

Being Imperial Regent has a hell of a lot of great, amazing and rather delightful benefits that I, Jack Blackheart, certainly enjoy most of the time. Especially, as I stood on the very top of the immense black metal Imperial Fortress with the icy cold wing slowly rubbing my cheeks dry.

I had always enjoyed the Fortress way too much actually. It was such a beacon of the Rex's immense power, authority and sheer brutality with its huge black 8-point star design that stretched on for thousands of miles in all directions and upwards even more.

It was next to impossible to look down below and see the charred black stone ground that so many soldiers walked over every day, because it was their duty to the Rex. I actually wanted to know if they did this out of choice but I doubted I could ever get a reliable answer.

The part of the fortress I was standing on had to be my favourite. I was north towards the largest city on Earth and it might have been miles upon miles away but it still looked great with its fiery spires reaching up into space and so many little beautiful lights of ships, shuttles and fighters buzzing around the city like bees.

The wind might have been icy cold scented with wonderful hints of jasmine, lavender and peanuts leaving the good taste of nature on my tongue but I honestly could have stayed out here for hours.

And that city was so damn beautiful.

On cold dark nights like this, it was something to behold and it just reminded me how great humanity could be. When I first joined the Rex, I was so filled with hope about the Imperium.

Of course back then I believe, I believed the Imperium was a force for good, change and the betterment of everyone. But that was a lie, probably the biggest lie in human history because the Imperium was all about control these days.

I was probably the most free person in the Imperium because I was the Rex's right and left hand but even I felt the imposing stare of security cameras from time to time. So I just admired the sheer beauty of the nearby city and just dreamed for a single moment that the people in the city might be free, laughing and smiling with each other.

Footsteps came up behind me and I dared to

imagine it was someone to save me.

I just had to smile at that idea because whenever I visited a place in the Imperium, I always donated Rexes, food and machinery to the local population just so they might have a better life, and maybe I could continue to believe in that small, small moment that the Imperium was a force for good once again.

I often argued with myself about leaving, running away and just abandoning the Rex to his crazy delusions of control and power but I didn't want to.

As stupid as it sounded this was still my home, the Rex had found me when I was a late teenager on the streets and starving so he bought me in, gave me food and shelter.

And I served him, happily at first and now I just press on because the work can be great at times.

"You're up late tonight, Lord Regent,"

I recognised the voice instantly. It was a deep female voice so I turned around and grinned at my old friend Perrigin, or Perry for short, in a great-looking blue dress, military boots and small gun in her hand. She still looked beautiful.

She was meant to be in charge of forcing the various Planetary Governors in the Imperium to the Rex's Will but she was so good at it that most of them didn't notice they were being manipulated. And most of the time Perry was just too much fun to be around.

But she looked serious tonight.

"I never knew you had a brother," Perry said not daring to look at me.

I frowned at her. I hadn't even thought of my brother for four decades, he had abandoned me when the Rex's forces invaded our settlement and killed our parents. It was the reason why I was on the streets and it was awful.

My brother had been a good man, a hard worker and a good fighter but whilst all the other men and women in our settlement rushed to fight the invaders. My brother ran. I screamed out his name. He ran even faster.

"Why?" I asked.

Perry shrugged. "I have a new prisoner to enjoy and he claims to be your brother,"

I had to nod at that. It was a hell of a story and I still didn't understand why the Rex "gifted" prisoners to Perry. I know that her mother was an expert interrogator but I doubted she had passed on the knowledge to Perry.

"You want me to talk to him then?" I asked, really hoping she would say no so I could continue to enjoy the view.

"Yes because if this is your brother then I want to know why he was sneaking about trying to assassinate the Rex," Perry said frowning.

A lump caught in my throat as I realised that if this was truly my brother then he was a dead man. As much as I too wanted the Rex dead, I certainly wasn't stupid enough to try.

He was too smart, too well protected and too

damn paranoid to ever allow an assassin within two miles of him. Let alone allow an assassin into his Fortress.

"Take me to him," I said.

Perry hugged me, grabbed me by the hand and she dragged me towards the prisoner.

This wasn't going to end well I knew that for sure.

***

One of the many foundational lies the Imperium is built on is that the Imperium is a type of democracy where the millions upon millions of planetary governors vote amongst themselves for who should have critical roles. Like the people in charge of the military, policing, security and so on.

It's all a lie because the Rex controls everything and every single bit of freedom a person believes they have is a carefully crafted lie by the Rex himself.

I was starting to understand that now.

I followed Perry into a massive stone domed chamber with rough grey walls and it was barely large enough to swing a cat inside, and as soon as I stepped inside the temperature dropped so much my breath formed thick columns of vapour.

It was a horrible feeling seeing the hairs on my arms shoot up like defences and small crystals of ice formed on me. The chamber looked like it was meant to be warm and cosy but nothing could be further from the truth.

There were no white-armoured guards or soldiers

in the chamber like I had seen in their thousands all over the Fortress. There was only a single man in the chamber with his cheeks and eyes swollen so much that I couldn't tell if this was my brother or not.

Sure the man had the same long raven black hair as my brother but it was burnt and ripped out in places, probably thanks to Perry.

The man's fingers were bleeding and shooting off in weird angles and I really didn't care to look at the rest of him.

I didn't have a cast-iron stomach like Perry clearly did.

My stomach twisted into a painful knot just looking at him so I focused on a small chipped spot on the domed wall behind him instead.

"You came then," he said in a course loving voice that my brother always used on me because he really did love me back in the day.

The lump from earlier returned stronger to my throat. I just couldn't believe this was my brother. The big brother that had taught me how to hack into a holo-system. The big brother that had cooked my dinners when our parents had to work late. The big brother that had loved me every moment of every day.

He was here and he was suffering.

"I came because it is my duty to the Rex," I said out of instinct.

My brother grinned. "Do you remember my

name brother?"

I nodded. "Jason,"

Perry smiled as she took out a massive dagger. "This dagger is way too clean for my liking so please tell me, who are you working for?"

I forced myself not to look in horror at my friend. She shouldn't be doing this, this was wrong on so many levels.

"I would rather die than tell you Rex scum," Jason said.

Perry laughed. She went to thrust the dagger into him but I grabbed her wrist.

Her eyes widened as we both realised what the hell I had just done and I seriously hoped that Perry was going to break her orders and training by not killing me immediately.

"I will get the information from him," I said hoping to buy myself some time. "If he still doesn't give me the information then you can flay him alive if you care,"

I didn't want that to happen but I wanted more time.

Perry nodded so I went down and knelt in front of my brother's twisted tortured form.

"Did you ever find a boyfriend?" I asked smiling. That was actually what I hoped had happened to him over the years, I hoped my big brother had found love, happiness and joy.

He frowned and looked at Perry. "She killed him two years ago,"

I nodded. "I'm sorry,"

At least that ruled out any romantic links being the people helping him but I didn't know what I was hoping to achieve by getting the information from him.

He was going to die unless I could magically come up with an idea to save the both of us. I was clever. I just doubted I was that clever.

"I won't tell you who's helping me," Jason said.

"But they'll kill you if you don't,"

"They're going to kill me anyway," he said and I knew he was lying.

"Then I can promise you they'll kill you faster and less painfully," I said looking at Perry.

She rolled her eyes like I had just taken the fun out of her playtime but she nodded.

I was about to take Jason's hands but then I realised how mutilated they were and how tortured the rest of his body was. I didn't dare touch him in case it caused him crippling pain.

"Please. You protected me a lot during school and my childhood. Let me repay the favour by helping you now," I said.

He shook his head. "Why do you work for them?"

And before I realised it I was replying out of instinct. "Because the Rex is the only one that can help humanity not descend into chaos, hatred and anarchy. He is the difference between freedom and chaos and control and safety,"

Jason laughed. "I will not tell you who helped me because there was no one. I don't work with the Keres and their magic, I don't work with the Enlightened Republic and I don't work with anyone else,"

I almost believed him because humanity hated the foul alien Keres with their freakish magic with a passion. I had met people from the independent and so-called free people of the Enlightened Republic and my brother didn't have the arrogance of them, but my brother had lied.

He had admitted he worked with people because Perry had killed his boyfriend two years ago.

"You worked with your boyfriend so who are you working with?" I asked. "I am Imperial Regent, I designed and reviewed the security plans of this Fortress myself almost daily. Unless you had inside help, it is impossible for you to do this,"

Then I looked at Perry and I frowned.

I reached for a weapon I normally carried but I was having it cleaned tonight as I was meeting the Rex tomorrow.

When I looked at Perry again she had a dagger pointed at me and I just shook my head. She was a traitorous bastard and then she clicked her fingers.

Jason screamed in agony as his bones, muscles and skin were ripped apart and reforged into the image of Jason's real form. He was tall, muscular and attractive like a university jock that all the girls gushed over. He looked perfect.

But I just couldn't believe that Perry had magic or something. I knew as Imperial Regent that it was a lie that no human could produce magic but the numbers were like 1 in every one trillion.

I had no idea that Perry had magic before now.

"So why this?" I asked.

"Because I knew you were a fake," Jason said. "My brother was a good man, he hated the Rex and he never would have attacked a woman trying to help me kill him. You have changed. You are one of his puppets,"

I shook my head and noticed there was a small red flashing light behind them and I sort of felt like I needed to make them confess.

It was a strange sensation but as soon as I thought about it I realised I was right. Yet if there was help coming to stop these assassins then I just wanted to make sure I didn't die in the process.

And the Rex's help was always conditional on me being loyal to him. If I showed any sign of weakness here then he would allow these two to kill me.

Before killing them himself.

"This isn't delusion Jason. This is just the truth. The truth is the Rex is the only person who could save humanity and that's a good person," I said not even forcing out the words.

Jason took a dagger out from his back. "I'm disappointed that you allowed yourself to believe in these lies,"

I shook my head. I had to find out what their plan was.

"And why you Perry?" I asked. "You were always good to the Rex and he rewarded you,"

"Because everything is a lie and everything will burn!" Perry shouted.

She charged at me.

I jumped back.

She swung again.

I punched her.

Jason tackled me.

Pinning me against the wall.

He whacked me round the face.

Forcing his blade against my throat.

"Why do this?" I asked. "What do you intend to achieve? Make us a democratic republic?"

"I would never allow us to become like the Enlightened Republic but Truth must happen," Perry said.

And then I realised exactly what had happened to her. My good friend Perry had simply allowed herself to think too much about reality, she questioned all the lies and propaganda and the foundations the Imperium was built on.

As Imperial Regent I often created the foundational lies and considered them, it was possible to know what was fact and what was fiction these days but reality was a lie.

Of course over the years it had destroyed my

mental health, I had been on the brink so many times of just wanting to annihilate it all because I just wanted the truth.

I had never jumped off the edge. Clearly Perry had.

I looked my brother dead in the eye. He didn't want to do this. He looked vulnerable.

I punched him.

He fell backwards.

I jumped forward.

Grabbing the dagger.

Snatching it out of his hand.

He charged at me.

I thrusted the blade into his chest.

Perry charged at me.

Screaming in emotional agony.

She wasn't focusing.

She swung her blade.

I ducked.

She rushed past me.

I leapt up.

Stabbing her in the back.

And as the Rex's personal white-armoured bodyguards stormed in, I just shook my head as I stared at the corpse of my dear big brother and I truly realised that these two were always going to die tonight.

Because every single freedom a person thought they had was a simple lie created by the Rex.

This was all a test and one I feared for my life that I had passed. I hoped.

***

The next morning I was standing at my most favourite spot on the immense stone fortress walls staring at the beautiful city in the distance. The bright morning was surprisingly warm, calm and the sun was strongly beaming down on me like a spotlight. The air was wonderfully fresh with hints of jasmine, lavender and pecans filling the air and I was so glad to be alive.

Last night might as well have been a blur for all the good that happened to me. The bodyguards had stormed in and chopped up the corpses to make sure my dear brother and Perry were well and truly dead and then the chunks were taken away.

I was left alone in the room for a few moments before I confidently walked out and I almost jumped out of my own skin at the imposing sight of the Rex in his jet-black, twisted, terrifying armour.

He didn't say anything to me. He only grinned, smiled and nodded like he had been proven right about me and maybe he had.

I had always believed that I was different to the rest of the Fortress, I believed that I was playing a long game against the Rex but maybe I wasn't anything that I thought I was. Maybe I really had become the lies, deceit and carefully crafted mould of what I was meant to be by the Rex's design.

And now I was thinking about it, maybe that wasn't a bad thing. Sure the Rex was a master of manipulation but he trusted me, wanted me to live and I was already the second most powerful person in the entire Imperium so maybe, just maybe I should start acting like it.

Of course I wouldn't take the galaxy for myself but maybe I could have all the power I desired and I could become something, someone completely different to the little boy who had lost his brother and parents.

Maybe I could become something far greater but simply allowing the Rex to remain in power for a little while longer, because there was a simple truth that everyone, even people as *smart* as the Rex, forgets and that is that every ruler falls in the end.

Every King, Emperor and Regent in human history has fallen at some point and when one of them falls there is something, someone to replace them.

And I'm fully determined to make sure when the Rex falls that I am the person to replace him and history will remember my name and there is a single word that will echo across the centuries as the person who took over the Imperium after the evil Rex had fallen.

I just smiled and allowed the warm sun to embrace me lovingly as I realised just how great the future could be, and I was really looking forward to how everyone would remember the simple name *Blackheart* in the bitter end.

FARMING RESTRICTIONS

Farming Director Adam Grant leant against the wonderfully warm balcony made from soft, sweet marble that was freshly shipped in from some random colony that he didn't care about. The soft refreshing, slightly warm breath brushed his cheeks and he was so looking forward to today.

His balcony was attached to an immense circular spaceship painted black that hovered just off the hard, cracked ground of Ceres 14. A beautifully lush planet most of the time but right now, that statement was in question.

For as far as Adam could see the ground was yellow, hard and cracked and it made no sense at all considering it rained twice a week on this planet, just as the glorious Rex had designed it. The latest data suggested the dryness of the planet was spreading a little too quickly for Adam's liking and sooner or later it would be impossible to grow crops on.

It was also strange and a little confusing that the large mountains and rolling hills of the planet that had been filled with olive trees, vegetables and more only yesterday were now completely empty, and the hills were mostly flat.

He supposed there could have been some kind of environmental reason for it all, but Adam had been working here for two decades now and this had never happened before. The environmental systems that destroyed the planet's natural weather systems were in perfect working order so all of this should have been impossible.

Adam really enjoyed the large, fat sun beaming down on him sending gentle warmth through his body and the sweet smells of corn, strawberries and honey filling the air from the latest harvest.

Possibly the last harvest for a long while.

Adam hated to imagine what Earth and the Rex would say when news of their crisis reached them. All Adam had wanted was a nice position of watching fruit, vegetables and livestock grow and he might have to do some paperwork from time to time but clearly he was actually going to have to do something.

He flat out hated the idea of that. And he hated the implications of the dryness of the planet even more. Everyone in the Imperium knew that the Rex only delivered food and water to planets that showed the most devotion to him and their dedication to rewrite history in his image.

It was only a month ago when he had been ordered to deliver two warships filled the most nutritious vegetables to reward a mining colony for killing all their history professors and over two thousand rebels who hated the Rex's rule.

Adam didn't agree with rewarding murder and bloodshed in the slightest but the Rex was the ruler of the Imperium and until anyone had the balls to rise up against him. Nothing would ever change in the Imperium.

And things would only continue to get worse and worse. Adam hated it how he had already been ordered to *decrease* food production by 20% over the past year to "give the populous of the Imperium more incentive to worship the Rex".

Adam's hands formed fists at the very notion of him not being able to do his job and actually have to make innocent people starve because of the Rex's twisted ideology. It was bad enough that the Imperium only allowed food to be grown on Farming Worlds that were highly, highly regulated but it was just stupid to have every single thing Adam did watched and approved by Earth.

Earth was just stupid.

"Chief," a woman said behind him.

Adam forced himself not to jump as the woman's voice sliced through the relaxing silence of the warm morning, he had wanted to enjoy the peace for a few more moments but that was never going to happen with a crisis unfolding around him.

Especially when he turned to face the woman and he was surprised she was wearing the black battle armour of the Imperial Army. Her medals and stripes and crowns on her armour told Adam everything he needed to know.

He was in the presence of one of the Imperium's high-ranking military officers. She was a Lord Commander, probably the Lord Commander of this entire sector of space and that never ended well.

As she came over to Adam and leant next to him, he had to admit with her long beautiful eyelashes, perfect smile and smooth skin she was certainly beautiful. Even her jasmine-scented perfume was a luxury Adam could never afford so why was a very rich and well-to-do commander visiting his little slice of hell?

"I was sent by Earth directly to investigate the matter of your planet," the woman said. "I am Lord Commander Isabella Coze,"

Adam forced himself not to frown as she said her name. Everyone, even the people living under rocks, knew of Commander Coze and how she enjoyed watching entire planets, races and populations get burnt alive for the smallest of infractions against the Imperium.

If she was here then his fate was already sealed. Not including the fate of all his workers, crops and the billions of people that relied on his food production.

"The Rex proposes that you have broken many Farming Restrictions and this is His Will and Plan to make you suffer," Coze said.

Adam shook his head. He knew that the Rex believed himself to be some kind of deranged god but he wasn't. And it was flat out impossible that Rex and his so-called divine power could reach through hundreds of thousands of solar systems to Ceres just to make the planet dry.

And if Coze believed it then she was a dick.

"I do not believe him," Coze said. "I believe there is a real cause to this planet's problems and whilst I am under rules to command you to build churches to the Rex. I am more concerned about my own military's food supply,"

Adam made sure his face didn't react because even Coze just admitting the Rex was wrong was more than enough to earn her a very slow, painful and agonising death.

"Where did the problems start?" Coze asked.

Adam shook his head. "They didn't. Everything just happened in front of my worker's eyes working the night shift last night. All three affected areas of the planet were impacted at once,"

Adam hated saying it out loud because it was like some strange personal failing but Coze was here now and he couldn't fail her. Otherwise everything he had ever wanted, built and aspired to would be obliterated and erased from history like every single thing in the Imperium was being.

"I'll take you to the largest impacted area now," Adam said and he walked away before Coze could answer.

He just hoped beyond hope this exploration would get everyone he cared about killed.

***

Adam was seriously surprised how difficult it was to get to the largest impacted area, it might have been on the other side of the planet but for some reason all the workers refused to go there. It also seemed like the machines and shuttles and drones refused to travel there either.

Adam wasn't sure if that had more to do with the drones and other pieces of technology being programmed to only travel to fertile ground, but it was still strange.

After two hours of trying to find a shuttle to take them there, Adam and Coze stepped off the black metal ramp of the circular shuttle and stood on the hard, cracked orange ground.

As the circular shuttle zoomed off into the distance like it was a child running away from a monster, Adam couldn't believe it as he stared out into the distance that stretched on for hundreds of miles, he just couldn't see anything but hard cracked flat land.

This was actually one of the most hilly areas of the planet and that made it perfect for growing grapes, grazing sheep and cows and even creating some genetic hybrids that the Rex said were illegal. Coze didn't need to know that of course.

But now Adam just couldn't believe how an

entire farming ecosystem that had been thriving for over twenty years had disappeared overnight and the impacted area was spreading.

The air smelt burnt, crispy and there was a strange undertone of charred flesh that made no sense too.

"What did your workers describe happened?" Coze asked.

Adam shrugged. "They reported working on a hill, picking grapes at night because it's cooler. Then the next moment they were on flat hard, cracked ground with no grapes in their baskets,"

Coze shook her head. "If this is a trick then I swear to you I will kill you,"

Adam shook a few steps away. "Why would I play a trick on you? I didn't even know I supplied the military with food,"

"You don't. At least not yet but the Rex is rearranging how the Imperium's food production works so your planet will become military-only food,"

Adam threw his arms up in the air. "What about all the billions of people that rely on my planet for food? We both know the Rex will not allow them to grow their own food and he will not offer them another Farming World as their source of food,"

Coze grinned. "At least I'm not the only traitor on this planet,"

Adam hardly believed himself to be a traitor to humanity just because he didn't agree with billions of people starving but maybe that was the key to solving this mystery.

Adam knelt down on the hot cracked ground and he was surprised how rough and almost razor sharp the ground was. None of this was natural and he had no idea who would have the technology to actually pull this off.

Except the Rex of course.

Adam looked at Coze. "Why is the Rex killing this planet?"

Coze shrugged. "Because… he isn't. He really isn't trying to kill you or the billions of planets that rely on you. He wants to kill me and my military planet,"

Adam smiled. He hadn't realised that the rumours were true, that the Imperial Army weren't stationed on normal planets and that they were actually stationed on their own planets. Probably some kind of military Fortress Planet.

"Why would he want to kill you?" Adam asked.

Coze looked up at the crystal clear sky for a moment before looking at Adam.

"Because I was wrong to follow the Rex and burn entire planets to the ground. The Rex is wrong and me and my planet have succeeded from the Imperium," she said.

Adam laughed. He had to admit that Lord Commander Coze was extremely ballsy and bold and stupid.

Everyone knew that no one just succeeded from

the Imperium without their planet being turned into a wasteland.

"I control two billion soldiers and this entire sector of space," Coze said. "Me turning my back on the Imperium is a massive blow that the Imperium will quickly recover from so me and my forces are fleeing towards the Enlightened Republic,"

Adam laughed. "That's a myth. The Enlightened Republic is simply a myth designed by the Rex to give people false hope,"

Coze grabbed his wrist. "No. It isn't. I encountered a Republic cell operating on my planet and I interrogated them. They showed me proof and they showed me that there was a better way to live,"

Adam wasn't buying it. It was impossible to imagine that there was a group of humans able to live in peace without the constant oversight of the Rex.

"They're a group of solar systems on the furthest reaches of the Imperium that encourage people to learn, vote for democracy and live freely without the control of the Rex,"

Adam waved his hands about. "How does this relate to what's going on on my planet?"

Coze frowned. "The Rex must have learnt that I would come here first before setting off so we would have enough food to make the journey. And I didn't want to burden the Republic when we arrived so I wanted enough food for us to survive for maybe a decade,"

Adam nodded that seemed perfectly reasonable

and it was an easy order to fulfil considering he normally sent enough food to last planets twenty or thirty years at a time.

Adam just shook his head as he watched a thin line of dust blew about in the wind and he found it hard to believe that two billion soldiers (a mere drop in the ocean of the Imperium's population and military might) was enough reason to justify destroying an entire Farming World that the Rex knew billions relied on for food.

That was murder to him and Adam had to admit that if the Enlighted Republic did exist then he certainly wanted to be apart of it.

He no longer wanted to live in an Imperium that had such discard for the lives of innocent humans that only wanted to feed themselves, their friends and most importantly their families.

***

Adam stood on an immense circular bridge of a bright white circular warship a few years later and he was just amazed as they entered the Enlightened Republic just how different it was.

They were thousands upon thousands of miles away from the border but the bright red, red and purple planets looked so magical and hopeful that Adam was so looking forward to the future.

He and Coze had become great friends over the past years, and Adam liked to think he had really helped her overcome her past and trauma about burning so many planets to ash. In all fairness she had hardly had a choice and she was only following her conditioning from the Rex.

He was that good at controlling people after all.

The bridge might have been empty with only the gentle hum of the engines keeping him company, but Adam liked how everyone in the fleet was enjoying their evening meals. And whilst he really hoped that the billions of people that relied on Ceres 14 had found another source of food, he still wasn't ashamed that as he, his staff and all of Coze's military lot emptied the planet of food to travel to the Enlightened Republic because it meant that they could help their new friends survive.

And Adam was no military man but he had a feeling that the Rex, his generals and spies were always watching, learning and studying the Enlightened Republic for the right moment to strike and claim it for themselves.

For any degree of peace, freedom or love in the galaxy was just a carefully crafted illusion by the Rex because he wanted humanity all to himself.

And he would never stop until all of humanity worshipped him and he controlled them all, but as long as Adam lived he was going to make sure that never ever happened and if making sure the Enlightened Republic had enough food was a way to do that, then he was perfectly happy with that.

WAY OF THE ODYSSEY SHORT STORY COLLECTION VOLUME 2

GET YOUR FREE SHORT STORY NOW!
And get signed up to Connor Whiteley's newsletter to hear about new gripping books, offers and exciting projects. (You'll never be sent spam)

https://www.subscribepage.io/garrosignup

About the author:

Connor Whiteley is the author of over 60 books in the sci-fi fantasy, nonfiction psychology and books for writer's genre and he is a Human Branding Speaker and Consultant.

He is a passionate warhammer 40,000 reader, psychology student and author.

Who narrates his own audiobooks and he hosts The Psychology World Podcast.

All whilst studying Psychology at the University of Kent, England.

Also, he was a former Explorer Scout where he gave a speech to the Maltese President in August 2018 and he attended Prince Charles' 70th Birthday Party at Buckingham Palace in May 2018.

Plus, he is a self-confessed coffee lover!

WAY OF THE ODYSSEY SHORT STORY COLLECTION VOLUME 2

Other books by Connor Whiteley:

Bettie English Private Eye Series
A Very Private Woman
The Russian Case
A Very Urgent Matter
A Case Most Personal
Trains, Scots and Private Eyes
The Federation Protects
Cops, Robbers and Private Eyes
Just Ask Bettie English
An Inheritance To Die For
The Death of Graham Adams
Bearing Witness
The Twelve
The Wrong Body
The Assassination Of Bettie English
Wining And Dying
Eight Hours
Uniformed Cabal
A Case Most Christmas

Gay Romance Novellas
Breaking, Nursing, Repairing A Broken Heart
Jacob And Daniel
Fallen For A Lie
Spying And Weddings
Clean Break

Awakening Love
Meeting A Country Man
Loving Prime Minister
Snowed In Love
Never Been Kissed
Love Betrays You

Lord of War Origin Trilogy:
Not Scared Of The Dark
Madness
Burn Them All

The Fireheart Fantasy Series
Heart of Fire
Heart of Lies
Heart of Prophecy
Heart of Bones
Heart of Fate

City of Assassins (Urban Fantasy)
City of Death
City of Marytrs
City of Pleasure
City of Power

WAY OF THE ODYSSEY SHORT STORY COLLECTION VOLUME 2

<u>Agents of The Emperor</u>
Return of The Ancient Ones
Vigilance
Angels of Fire
Kingmaker
The Eight
The Lost Generation
Hunt
Emperor's Council
Speaker of Treachery
Birth Of The Empire
Terraforma
Spaceguard

<u>The Rising Augusta Fantasy Adventure Series</u>
Rise To Power
Rising Walls
Rising Force
Rising Realm

<u>Lord Of War Trilogy (Agents of The Emperor)</u>
Not Scared Of The Dark
Madness
Burn It All Down

Miscellaneous:
RETURN
FREEDOM
SALVATION
Reflection of Mount Flame
The Masked One
The Great Deer
English Independence

OTHER SHORT STORIES BY CONNOR WHITELEY

Mystery Short Story Collections

Criminally Good Stories Volume 1: 20 Detective Mystery Short Stories

Criminally Good Stories Volume 2: 20 Private Investigator Short Stories

Criminally Good Stories Volume 3: 20 Crime Fiction Short Stories

Criminally Good Stories Volume 4: 20 Science Fiction and Fantasy Mystery Short Stories

Criminally Good Stories Volume 5: 20 Romantic Suspense Short Stories

WAY OF THE ODYSSEY SHORT STORY COLLECTION VOLUME 2

<u>Mystery Short Stories:</u>
Protecting The Woman She Hated
Finding A Royal Friend
Our Woman In Paris
Corrupt Driving
A Prime Assassination
Jubilee Thief
Jubilee, Terror, Celebrations
Negative Jubilation
Ghostly Jubilation
Killing For Womenkind
A Snowy Death
Miracle Of Death
A Spy In Rome
The 12:30 To St Pancreas
A Country In Trouble
A Smokey Way To Go
A Spicy Way To GO
A Marketing Way To Go
A Missing Way To Go
A Showering Way To Go
Poison In The Candy Cane
Kendra Detective Mystery Collection Volume 1
Kendra Detective Mystery Collection Volume 2
Mystery Short Story Collection Volume 1

Mystery Short Story Collection Volume 2
Criminal Performance
Candy Detectives
Key To Birth In The Past

<u>Science Fiction Short Stories:</u>
Their Brave New World
Gummy Bear Detective
The Candy Detective
What Candies Fear
The Blurred Image
Shattered Legions
The First Rememberer
Life of A Rememberer
System of Wonder
Lifesaver
Remarkable Way She Died
The Interrogation of Annabella Stormic
Blade of The Emperor
Arbiter's Truth
Computation of Battle
Old One's Wrath
Puppets and Masters
Ship of Plague
Interrogation
Edge of Failure

WAY OF THE ODYSSEY SHORT STORY COLLECTION VOLUME 2

<u>Fantasy Short Stories:</u>
City of Snow
City of Light
City of Vengeance
Dragons, Goats and Kingdom
Smog The Pathetic Dragon
Don't Go In The Shed
The Tomato Saver
The Remarkable Way She Died
Dragon Coins
Dragon Tea
Dragon Rider

<u>All books in 'An Introductory Series':</u>
Clinical Psychology and Transgender Clients
Clinical Psychology
Careers In Psychology
Psychology of Suicide
Dementia Psychology
Clinical Psychology Reflections Volume 4
Forensic Psychology of Terrorism And Hostage-Taking
Forensic Psychology of False Allegations
Year In Psychology
CBT For Anxiety
CBT For Depression
Applied Psychology

BIOLOGICAL PSYCHOLOGY 3RD EDITION
COGNITIVE PSYCHOLOGY THIRD EDITION
SOCIAL PSYCHOLOGY- 3RD EDITION
ABNORMAL PSYCHOLOGY 3RD EDITION
PSYCHOLOGY OF RELATIONSHIPS- 3RD EDITION
DEVELOPMENTAL PSYCHOLOGY 3RD EDITION
HEALTH PSYCHOLOGY
RESEARCH IN PSYCHOLOGY
A GUIDE TO MENTAL HEALTH AND TREATMENT AROUND THE WORLD- A GLOBAL LOOK AT DEPRESSION
FORENSIC PSYCHOLOGY
THE FORENSIC PSYCHOLOGY OF THEFT, BURGLARY AND OTHER CRIMES AGAINST PROPERTY
CRIMINAL PROFILING: A FORENSIC PSYCHOLOGY GUIDE TO FBI PROFILING AND GEOGRAPHICAL AND STATISTICAL PROFILING.
CLINICAL PSYCHOLOGY
FORMULATION IN PSYCHOTHERAPY
PERSONALITY PSYCHOLOGY AND

WAY OF THE ODYSSEY SHORT STORY COLLECTION VOLUME 2

INDIVIDUAL DIFFERENCES
CLINICAL PSYCHOLOGY REFLECTIONS VOLUME 1
CLINICAL PSYCHOLOGY REFLECTIONS VOLUME 2
Clinical Psychology Reflections Volume 3
CULT PSYCHOLOGY
Police Psychology

A Psychology Student's Guide To University
How Does University Work?
A Student's Guide To University And Learning
University Mental Health and Mindset

www.ingramcontent.com/pod-product-compliance
Lightning Source LLC
LaVergne TN
LVHW011855060526
838200LV00054B/4341